RIPPLES

Three stories that stimulate the mind
and weave a tapestry of human emotions and events

Douglas W. Warner

1st WORLD
PUBLISHING

RIPPLES

Three stories that stimulate the mind
and weave a tapestry of human emotions and events

Douglas W. Warner

© Douglas W. Warner 2010

Published by 1stWorld Publishing
P.O. Box 2211, Fairfield, Iowa 52556
tel: 641-209-5000 • fax: 866-440-5234
web: www.1stworldpublishing.com

First Edition

LCCN: 2010939825
SoftCover ISBN: 978-1-4218-9183-5
HardCover ISBN: 978-1-4218-9184-2
eBook ISBN: 978-1-4218-9185-9

DEDICATION

To my wife, Shirley, who decided that I should write
instead of retire.

To Shirley and Tamra who read and edited my work.

To Nathaniel, Katy, Dylan and Grant who always
want to hear a story.

.

FORWARD

Just about everyone has heard about the "butterfly effect," the theory that wind caused by the beat of a butterfly's wing can be the beginning of a storm. I suppose it's true, but I'm not sure if little things make big things happen or if big happenings "ripple" many little things.

The three stories you are about to read explore the relationships between human decisions and events, or, perhaps, the influence of events on human decisions.

I hope these stories cause you to think and ponder thoughts that are outside of the box. Hopefully, you will experience the "rippling effect."

Douglas W. Warner

THE EVENT

CHAPTER ONE
SILAS

Silas preached his first sermon when he was sixteen years old. This Sunday morning would be his last.

When Silas was sixteen, the deacons of the small rural church where Silas and his mother attended decided it would be good to encourage the younger boys to participate in worship services. Silas was asked to bring a message on a Sunday evening, and he accepted before he learned that the other two boys asked to participate had bowed out.

After a month of planning and having sought advice from the minister, several deacons, and his Mama, Silas was ready. He felt sure that his many pages of notes, with verses, quotes, and stories would help him through the pending ordeal.

The Sunday finally came, and following the usual songs and prayers the congregation of one hundred and twelve grew silent as Silas nervously mounted the pulpit.

To this day, Silas cannot remember what happened. He can remember fear; he can remember the taste of metal. He remembers sounds coming out of his mouth, but the words were tangled and twisted by his paralyzed tongue. He remembers pages of notes falling to the floor, and mostly, he remembers that death would be a welcomed relief.

Finally, as Silas finished reading his last page, he quickly stepped down from the pulpit and looked for a pew to hide under. When he glanced at his watch he realized that only seven minutes had passed from the time he had started the nerve racking ordeal, and all Silas could think was, "Never again, no, never again." As the last song was sung and a quick prayer offered, the service was over and Silas looked for the exit; but quickly, to Silas' surprise, people were gathering around him and praising his performance. With pats on the shoulder and kisses on the cheek Silas was smothered with praise and adoration. Then Silas' great aunt, Ammoreta, slowly approached Silas, and all the people gathered around gave ground to the richest lady in the congregation. Aunt Ammoreta had spoken to Silas only three times in his life, as he could remember, and he had never been to her house or she to his.

Aunt Ammoreta cupped her hands around Silas' face and kissed him on the forehead. Then backing up a little and looking Silas straight in the eyes, tears began to appear in her eyes. "Silas," she said, "God has called you to preach. Do not fail us!"

Silas was stunned. Never, never in his whole life had people showed such attention to him. Now everyone, including Aunt Ammoreta, was bathing him in praise. He was washed by a wave of joy and excitement, and then and there Silas made a declaration, "I have been called to preach!"

Two years passed and Silas had performed well enough in school that he could have gone to the local state college after graduation. However, Aunt Ammoreta, with her financial support and spiritual influence, had convinced Silas that a state university would only steal his Christian soul. After all, the state school taught evolution, situational ethics, and was generally morally defunct. Aunt Ammoreta made it clear that she would help Silas go to a school of preaching where a firm indoctrination of scripture, a full understanding of the requirements for salvation, and other general preaching skills would prepare him for a life time of service. It all sounded good to Silas, especially when Aunt Ammoreta threw in a car for him to use while commuting from the preacher training school to his home church where he would serve as a minister's helper and building custodian.

Three years passed quickly and Silas had proven himself a good student. He had read the Bible through five times and had memorized the more pertinent scriptures and how they were to be interpreted. When certifications of ordination were awarded, Silas had been honored with a place at the front of the line because he was first in his class of seven. Silas was twenty-one years old, certified to be a minister and anxious to put his hand to the plow of salvation.

Silas sent dozens of letters to congregations along with a copy of his credentials. Some of the congregations responded with a request for sermon tapes or videos. With great enthusiasm Silas would send his best sermons and anxiously wait for the call, but as the months passed and no congregation extended a "calling", Silas' enthusiasm was slowly leached by each rejection.

In addition to serving as custodian to his home congregation, Silas applied and obtained the job of driving a school bus to help meet his financial obligations that were stacking quickly. It seems that Aunt Ammoreta felt that paying Silas' tuition to the preaching school was sufficient and that additional help would not be prudent. As Aunt Ammoreta said, "God will do the rest"; and, of course at the time, Silas thought so too. Now, however, with his financial obligations mounting, he wasn't so sure. Silas applied for other jobs. He contacted the school system, but they rejected him for lack of credentials. He applied at Wal-Mart, but was rejected for lack of experience. Finally, Silas got a little relief by taking on a paper route. He would drive to Austin, some fifty miles away, get bundles of papers and deliver them to rural stores. Some weeks the pay was helpful, but too often he ended up spending his paper route profit on automobile repairs. As Silas celebrated his twenty-third birthday, he just didn't know how much longer he could last.

Silas' future took a turn when the current minister of the congregation announced that he was retiring to the farm. "Surely," Silas thought, "I am the logical pick for his replacement. I'm trained, I know the congregation, they know me, and I'm here!"

It was with no little excitement that Silas received notice from the deacons that they wanted to talk with him. He was sure that his time had arrived and he went to the meeting with great anticipation. However, shortly into the discussion Silas began to realize that matters were not developing the way he had dreamed. It seemed the deacons felt that he needed "a little more seasoning before he would be ready for the tasks of being head minister." Worse, the new minister that the deacons were considering needed more money than the congregation had been paying. The deacons felt that they could no longer support both Silas and the new minister, and they encouraged him to seek a calling from another congregation. However, the deacons did reiterate their belief that Silas had a great future, and they assured him that the congregation would continue to support him for ninety days.

Silas moved home with his mother, and after ninety days he found that his only means of support was working as a school bus driver, a newspaper deliverer, and part-time clerk at the local all-night gas and shop store. Within six months, Silas had to move from his mother's apartment. Seems her newly acquired boyfriend did not like to hear the ravings of Silas relative to their state of sin by living together.

Silas was twenty five years of age and working the late shift at the gas and shop store when a man entered the store one evening and stated that he had been looking for Silas. The man was a deacon for a small congregation some twenty miles to the east called Dowville, and they were looking for a preacher.

Two months later Silas had given up all his previous jobs and had accepted the calling to be the minister of the Dowville Church of God.

For Silas, the next three years were wonderful. He taught Sunday morning Bible class, preached the morning and evening services and taught again on Wednesday night. With a congregation of 163, Silas could make his visits with the sick and shut-ins in a matter of hours leaving him with plenty of time to fish, hunt, and prepare his lessons.

One Sunday afternoon Silas was invited to speak at a youth rally in a nearby town. While there, he met Lea. Lea had just graduated from high school and had gone to work for the local lumber company. They hit it off immediately and Silas had a new interest.

After a whirlwind courtship and with the blessing of Lea's folks—after all, Silas was a minister—Silas and Lea were married and moved into the trailer provided to him by the congregation; the trailer was located just behind the church building. She kept her job with the lumber company and with two incomes they were able to make ends meet.

As Silas neared the end of his third year with the Dowville Church of God, the deacons called for the annual meeting to discuss the coming year and salary arrangements. Of course, Silas was hoping for a slight raise so one could imagine how surprised he was when the deacons announced that it was time for Silas to seek a new calling. When he ask what their thinking was, the only thing the deacons would say was, "Your ministry just isn't a good fit for us." After assuring Silas of their love and best wishes for him and Lea in the future, he was granted four months in the trailer before the new minister would be arriving.

Silas and Lea moved in with her folks, but the arrangement did not set well with Lea or her parents. Each day Lea would go to work at the lumber mill, and Silas would work on his sermons. Soon, Lea's folks wanted financial help to cover the costs of their food and lodging, and each day Lea's resentment grew as she felt she wasn't appreciated for being the primary financial provider. Finally, after about six months, Lea decided that she had made a great mistake in marrying Silas. She liked the idea of marrying a minister, but the reality proved short of expectations. In short, Lea wanted a divorce, and Silas was asked to leave the house.

Before his breakup with Lea, Silas heard of a part time job as a minister for the Luder Fellowship Church located some eighteen miles to the west of Dowville. The Luder congregation had 87 members and an apartment attached to the building. He knew the congregation could not pay enough to support him, but he agreed to serve if the congregation would allow him to stay in the apartment and pay him what they could.

Of course the deacons wanted to know about Lea and the marriage, but after Silas explained that he loved Lea dearly and would always be faithful to her regardless of her worldly ways, they were satisfied that he had scriptural grounds for his conduct, and they extended a call to Silas to be the full-time minister of the Luder Fellowship Church. With Silas renewing his employment as a school bus driver as well as his newspaper delivery job, he made enough money to get by.

By the time Silas reached the age of thirty-five, he had served as the minister of five different congregations. All the congregations were located in rural areas and all were small in membership. But, no matter how hard Silas tried, within three or four years, he was told that his services were no longer needed.

Understand, Silas was a good man. There was nothing inherently wrong with him. Silas' problems stemmed from the core training received at the school of preaching and his lack of people skills. He was young when he entered the training school and lacked the necessary experience required to balance knowledge with wisdom. True, Silas had memorized many scriptures, but he didn't always know when to remain silent or which scripture would be most appropriate. For instance, on one occasion he was standing next to a mother who was gazing into the casket of her small daughter and sobbingly spoke, "I guess God took her home because He loved her so." Silas immediately felt compelled to explain God's love by reciting John 3:16. Now, of course, John 3:16 is a fine passage, but not totally appropriate for the occasion.

Silas had been taught and took to heart the belief that for all occasions the minister should have a brief homily. Too often, he spoke instead of listening. Oh, it wasn't that Silas could not sympathize with other people's problems. It was that he never developed true empathy for others. He knew when others were in pain and he wanted to help them, but his response, more often than not, was a verse designed to "perk-up" the bereaved.

Yes, Silas was a good man. He was morally virtuous and believed deeply in the existence of God. The problem was he believed that being good, virtuous, and accepting God was enough; yet, therein laid the seed of Silas' failure. He believed that the key to Christian faith was virtue; he never learned that the true key to God is love.

The weeks, months, and years took wing and Silas spent his time moving and serving as a minister as best he knew how. Thirty more years passed, fourteen different congregations, and Silas found himself at the age of sixty-five serving the People's Fellowship Church in Eatton.

Silas never remarried and never again saw his former wife. He believed that his innocence relative to his broken marriage was proven by his permanent single status.

Now, as a minister with over forty years of experience, one would have thought that Silas would have been well prepared for any occasion that could surface in a deacons' meeting, but again he was taken by surprise when he heard the head deacon say, "We have decided it would be best if you looked for a call from another congregation."

Something happened to Silas. Something snapped like a rubber band, but the snapping was not the result of too much stretch; it was caused by the rubber band becoming too brittle. He knew that this was the end to his ministry. "Enough!" Silas thought, "I cannot do this anymore." But, to the deacons he expressed understanding and the hope that they would find the man they needed. Silas assured them, "I will be out by the end of the month."

The last Sunday of the month came quickly. Silas had

spent three weeks preparing for his final sermon. In this case, "final" did not just mean the last sermon preached at this congregation. For him, this was the last sermon he would ever preach. This lesson would be Silas' final homily.

As the last song was sung and the congregation settled into a silent state for listening, Silas approached the pulpit to deliver his last sermon. "I have chosen as my last sermon to this congregation words to live by. My lesson today is entitled 'Our Untouchable God'".

CHAPTER TWO
MILTON

Milton was told by his mother, Sara, that he was named after her father, but Milton seldom saw his grandfather because he had been born out of wedlock and Sara and her father were estranged. So as for a birth father, the matter was mentioned but never discussed.

As one might conclude, Sara and Milton were poor and mostly alone. He remembers his mother's favorite saying, "It's just you and me against the world." One wonders why a mother would tell a child such a thing. Maybe for the mother it sounded strong or unifying, but to a child it simply means "we're alone," and being alone is a very scary thing for any child.

While Milton grew up in a single parent family, his physical skills soon won the admirations of his peers and coaches. Milton was husky and strong for his age and could run faster than most of the other boys. Once school started, Milton's social status was determined by the fact that he was always one of the best athletes in the school.

By the time Milton entered high school he was well known by the small community. Since junior high Milton had proven to be an unstoppable fullback in football with a unique record; Milton had never lost a yard on any carry of the ball; Milton was a star. He lettered three years in football and rushed for over a thousand yards in both his junior and senior years. Though Milton's academic performance did not match his athletic skills, his grades were good enough that he was offered athletic scholarships from two different state universities.

He would have made it to college had it not been for an embarrassing development. Milton's popularity was matched with a promiscuous sex life. Milton liked the girls and enjoyed the attention that came with his athletic skills, and the girls liked Milton. Then, the inevitable happened. Two weeks before Thanksgiving, Milton's girlfriend, Bonnie Lee, reported that she was pregnant.

For the next six weeks, Milton, his mother, Bonnie Lee, and her family discussed the options. Bonnie Lee and her folks were Catholics and an abortion was out of the question. When all had been said, it was decided that Milton and Bonnie Lee would secretly get married right after New Year's Day. They would move in with her parents, announce the marriage when she could no longer hide her condition or when it was learned that they were living together, finish high school, and have the baby in late July.

The plan might have worked, but soon Bonnie Lee's dad and Milton were at each other like raging bulls. The dad constantly muttered, "This punk knocked-up my daughter!", and Milton would raise his fist in challenge, "Let's step into the yard and settle this." By March the tension in the house was no longer bearable. Milton convinced Bonnie Lee that it would be better for them to move to an apartment.

For a time family relations seemed to get better. Milton got a night job at a fast food restaurant and Bonnie Lee tried to become a homemaker while both continued in school. Soon financial matters worsened and they began to fight constantly. Milton refused to borrow from her dad, and Bonnie Lee argued that his pride prevented her from having the things in life to which she was accustomed.

The end of May brought both tragedy and triumph. Both Milton and Bonnie Lee graduated from high school; that was the triumph, but the tragedy was life shattering. Milton had graduated, but his grades had fallen below the cut-off score required for an athletic scholarship. Without a scholarship, college was out of the question.

With the help of some of his friends, Milton was able to land a full-time job working in the oil fields; he became an assistant driver on an oil field vac-truck. The hours were long, but the money was much improved. The same could not be said about the relations between Milton and Bonnie Lee.

Although he was making more money and financial disaster had been averted, there still was not enough money to allow her to shop as she was accustomed. Most of the time, Bonnie Lee was unhappy. The apartment was too small; she didn't like being fat and pregnant; Milton was never home; life in general was not fun anymore.

For those who had been paying attention, it was neither a surprise nor unexpected when she moved back home in July and filed for divorce one week after the baby was born.

Two months later, even before the divorce was final, Milton joined the navy, to be gone for six years.

In the navy, Milton never served on a ship. After training he was stationed outside of San Diego and served as a machinist. He learned how to repair and build all kinds of steam and liquid pressure valves that were used in the engines of ships. He was good at his job and developed skills that would serve him well. All during the time Milton was in the service, he visited home once. He returned home only to bury his mother who had died in an automobile accident. While home for the funeral he was denied his request to see Bonnie Lee or the baby.

While Milton was serving in the navy, Bonnie Lee remarried and asked Milton to sign papers that would allow her new husband to adopt Sara, their daughter. Milton agreed because he had no contact with Bonnie Lee or Sara and because he knew that the adoption would remove him from child support payments.

After six years in active service, Milton was released to finish out his time in the reserves. He returned home having nowhere better to go and because he had the promise of a job working in the oil fields. This time, as a result of his navy training, Milton was made an assistant crew chief for developing and maintaining pipe routing from the well head to storage tanks.

During the next ten years, three issues drove Milton. Foremost, he wanted to enjoy life without responsibilities, a skill he easily mastered. He dated many women, but would commit to no one. He was fun to be around and all the guys who worked with him thought he was a great guy. He would give you the shirt off his back, but he did not want to commit to anything or anyone, with one exception.

Milton wanted a relationship with his daughter Sara. At first Bonnie Lee was totally against the idea, but as time passed he was allowed an occasional visit, having assured Bonnie Lee that he did not want her to worry about his involvement with Sara. He just wanted Sara to know that he cared about her.

The last issue of concern to Milton was the design and construction of a unique pressure valve that would bleed and capture gas while maintaining liquid flow. With his experience in the navy with steam and water he could nearly envision the valve, but adopting it to the oil fields would require a more rugged and sturdy design.

In the evenings, Milton started visiting a local machine shop and began to materialize his gas/liquid pressure valve. After several months of development, experiments, redesign, rework, and redevelopment, he emerged from the machine shop with his master piece. He called it the "G-L-P Valve."

After filing for a patent on his valve, Milton began to promote its uses in the field. At first, he provided the valve to his employer for free, just for testing, but when testing was complete and Milton started charging for the valve, problems arose with his employer. The oil company claimed that the valve was a product of work since he worked for the company, and therefore, the valve belonged to them. He got his own lawyer and quickly proved that the valve was his and as retribution to the oil company, Milton quadrupled the price of the valve. To his surprise, orders, hundreds of orders for the G-L-P Valve began to arrive. He bought the machine shop where he had developed the valve, hired the previous owner as the manager over operations and started producing in mass. Soon Milton was a wealthy man.

By the time Milton was thirty-five, he was financially fixed for life. However, domestically, matters were not going as well. Sara was now sixteen years old and had run away from home twice. On both occasions, Sara ended up at Milton's house begging him to let her stay. Milton was flattered by the request and Bonnie Lee, looking for help and relief, agreed to the arrangement.

Sara took advantage of the arrangement. With a little enticing, Milton provided Sara with new cloths, a new car, a credit card and even a lab puppy Sara named Chip. It wasn't long before Milton began to realize the folly of his ways; Sara maxed out her credit card three months in a row and started staying out late or overnight without permission. When he tried to talk with her about her conduct or spending, Sara would go into a crying rage and lock herself in her room. Finally, when he refused to grant her request to have her own apartment, Sara stormed out of the house for the last time.

Sara disappeared for a time and neither Milton nor Bonnie Lee could find her. Bonnie Lee filed a missing person report with the police, and Milton placed a trace on the credit card hoping to make contact, but nothing, nothing for three weeks. Then the call came, that call that all parents fear. Sara had been found and she was dead. The police had raided a drug house and found Sara's decomposed body out back in a storage room. She had been dead for two or three weeks.

Bonnie Lee blamed Milton, and he blamed himself. When Bonnie Lee told Milton, "Just go away, go away forever!", he took it literally. He sold his house and furnishings, made arrangements for his investments and business, bought a pick-up truck, grabbed Chip, Sara's dog, and set out for places unknown. Milton did not know where he was going; he was simply running.

For the next dozen years Milton was an American Gypsy. Sometimes staying a day, sometimes staying several months, he migrated from north to south, east to west. Most of the time he would stay in motels, but sometimes he would find a condo or timeshare housing. Hunting, fishing, and talking to folks became Milton's staples for living. He soon began to realize that talking to people and helping them, when he could, was what he liked most.

Slowly, without his cognitive awareness, Milton began to change. He had always been sociable and enjoyed people, but now he was learning to truly care about people, taking the time to help them as best he knew how. At first he thought money was the solution for all problems, but experiences taught him that money was a poor substitute for lasting assistance. He learned the old adage, "Buy a man a meal and he will be hungry again; teach him to fish and he will never starve." Oh, there were times when money did work: electricity turned off, auto parts and repairs needed, eye glasses, dental work; but with the passage of time, he learned to listen, and in the process, Milton, himself, changed.

When Milton first started traveling, he stuck to the large cities, but later he began to find joy in visiting the rural areas and relishing the flavor of the country folks. While he had not considered himself a religious man, he found he enjoyed the folksy ways of small, rural congregations, and especially loved their singing though it sometimes sounded like a mixture of howling dogs and peacocks. The sound was somewhat humorous, but their sincerity was above dispute.

It was the last Sunday of the month. Milton and Chip had gotten up early and were taking the back roads to an area reported to have great fishing. As he passed through a small town called Eatton that would normally go unnoticed, he saw a small white church building with a few cars parked out front. He looked at his watch and realized services had begun as he read the sign, "No strangers at our services; Services begin at 10:30." Milton decided to pull in and enjoy the singing. Leaving Chip in the truck with the windows down, he entered the auditorium as the last song was being sung and the congregation settled into a silent state for listening. Silas, the minister, approached the pulpit to deliver his last sermon. "I have chosen as my last sermon to this congregation words to live by. My lesson today is entitled 'Our Untouchable God.'"

CHAPTER THREE
EMMA

Emma was eleven years old and lived with her mother, Nancy, and grandmother, Nora. They lived in the small town of Eatton located in the Hill Country of Texas. Folks who lived in the area who weren't ranchers usually commuted to Austin or one of the other larger cities in order to find work. However, Nancy was a teacher's helper in the local school system, and Nora stayed at home to take care of Emma and to home school her.

Emma was a pretty child. Her face was round and her brown hair was usually in a ponytail. Her big brown eyes and pronounced dimples were more readily noticed than her frail body. For her age, she was small, looking more like an eight year old than a pre-teen. A second look revealed that Emma was handicapped.

When she was four years old, Emma was hit by an auto-mobile that was backing out of a driveway. As a result of the accident, she could not walk without steel braces on both of her legs. Even with the braces, she had to be assisted by either Nancy or Nora. Sometimes, on rare occasions, they would allow Emma to use a wheelchair, but not often. Both Nancy and Nora hoped, in spite of what doctors said, that someday she would walk without braces.

The most consistent event of the week was going to church on Sunday morning. Like clock-work, Nancy or Nora would help Emma to Bible study so she could be with the other three children who attended the class. Then, between Bible study and morning worship, Nancy or Nora would assist Emma with a stop at the bathroom. Each time Emma would always say she did not need to stop at the bathroom, and each visit would be accompanied with a lecture, "Emma, you go! And this time, we will not get up in church to go again!"

However, it did not matter what was said, the one thing you could count on was Emma needing to go to the bathroom during church. It wasn't that she had a bladder problem; to her it was a ritual distraction from sitting in the auditorium, and the ritual had been going on for years.

Of course, some of the good deacons suggested from time to time that maybe Nancy, Nora, and Emma would be better served if they sat closer to the back so that Emma's coming and going would be less noticed during services, but Nancy and Nora had picked their pew and to move was unthinkable. After all, there was a certain level of notoriety associated with going up and down the aisle each week.

It was the last Sunday of the month. Nancy had gotten up first that morning and prepared breakfast. Nora had finished her time in the bathroom and had helped Emma with her needs. Breakfast had been abbreviated as was the case every Sunday morning. There was never enough time to get everyone dressed and organized. As usual, there was the last rush to the car as they encouraged Emma to, "Pick up the pace."

A short ride and an assisted walk to a portable building

used for children's Bible class, and Emma was deposited for the next forty-five minutes with her friends and teacher. It was during class time that Nancy and Nora could have fellowship with their friends.

When Bible class ended, Nancy told Nora that she would get Emma so Nora could continue visiting. As usual Nancy took Emma to the bathroom, and though Emma swore that she did not need to go, Nancy demanded, "Emma, you go! And this time, we will not get up in church to go again!" Emma smiled knowing that the game would be played out again.

Emma enjoyed the singing so when church services started she was all ears for a while. After a song or two, someone would get up and lead a prayer. To her, Sunday morning prayers were pot-luck: sometimes short, sometimes long. Sometimes the prayers were funny like when Deacon Lou said, "Help Sister Ima with her bad case of constipation," or when Deacon Glen prayed for "all those present, living or dead."

Yes, Emma enjoyed the singing and sometimes the praying, but when the minister finally entered the pulpit she knew that it was time to start the game. After a few minutes into the sermon, she would lean over to Nora and say, "I need to go!" Nora would give Emma the usual stern look and then look over to Nancy who would also project a look of disapproval.

Then, Emma would begin the squirming session. She would twist back and forth as a sign of discomfort. When an appropriate about of squirming had taken place, she would proclaim, "I really need to go and I feel it coming!"

This would usually do it. Nancy or Nora would squint

their eyes as in anger, step into the aisle, assist Emma out of the pew and start the journey to the back. The trip would take about ten minutes, long enough to break the monotony of another Sunday morning sermon.

So, as Emma emerged from the bathroom and headed for the auditorium, she knew what was in store. The game would be played again today.

After the usual singing and praying, the congregation settled into a silent state for listening as Silas, the minister, mounted the pulpit. "I have chosen as my last sermon to this congregation words to live by. My lesson today is entitled 'Our Untouchable God.'"

CHAPTER FOUR
THE SERMON

As the last song was finished, the congregation settled into a silent state for listening. Silas walked to the pulpit climbing two steps and then rocked back and forth on his feet a couple of times trying to get comfortable in the pulpit, something he had never accomplished. Silas began slowly, "I have chosen as my last sermon to this congregation words to live by. My lesson today is entitled 'Our Untouchable God'".

He continued, "First I must tell you, God is holy! And, holy is neither an attribute nor a disposition. Holy is a state in which all the attributes and dispositions of the subject make the subject majestically awesome or divine!"

Silas went on to explain that the divine power of God gives Him omnipotence, that God's divine knowledge gives Him omniscience, and that God's divine presence gives Him omnipresence. Silas made it clear, "God is that being for which nothing more perfect or greater can be conceived." In essence, whatever a person can think about God is not enough. To Silas, God is beyond conception. Thus Silas, in all that he said and presented, made his case. Indeed, God is "untouchable."

Understand, Silas is sincere and nothing he said was

wrong. Jeremiah confirms that "Nothing is too hard for God," and the Psalms tells us that "there is no where one can go to hide from God," and that "His understanding has no limits." For certain, God is holy, but for anyone who already believes in God the matter of God's greatness or goodness need not be debated. For over forty five years Silas had been "preaching to the choir."

The key to Silas' spiritual mentality was found in his opening remark: "I have chosen as my last sermon to this congregation words to live by." Since preacher training school he had been taught and continued to believe that the role of the minister was to provide, on all occasions, "words to live by." While he had served up thousands and thousands of words over the years, he had yet to comprehend his basic failure to communicate.

Words are not enough. Words are a poor substitute for behavior; words do not instill love, or faith, or trust. Words are but sounds that come from the mouth, and they have little meaning until they are authenticated by actions. Silas had yet to learn that a minister, or any person, is not measured by the words he has said, but by the love he offers. Silas had spent his entire ministry always looking for the appropriate word, and in so doing most often missed the opportunity to simply feel the emotion of love, concern, and empathy.

No, Silas was not wrong in what he said. He was wrong in not believing, taking to heart, and acting on the words spoken.

Perhaps it wasn't his fault. Perhaps he did not realize that deep down he was angry with God.

For Silas' life had been one long test of enduring the suffering of a broken personal life and work situations that kept him on the brink of financial disaster. Yet, all the while he had to keep on smiling and declaring that "all things work for good for those who love the Lord." Yes, deep down he was angry with God, but he could not dare confess to others or himself such feelings.

Silas had yet to learn that a person does not have to accept God. One cannot be "brow beaten" into submission or threatened with the horror of a painful after-life.

Silas had yet to learn that Man's surrender to God cannot be based upon the blessings that are bestowed or promised or the pain of suffering if he should fail to do so. The very thought implies a scale, as if Man measures his blessings against the agonies of life and commits to the best offer. No, Man will only surrender to God when he knows in his heart that God loves him.

However, it didn't matter where Silas was going with his sermon. This Sunday, his lesson would end before it reached its predictable conclusion.

As Silas was completing his thoughts on the attributes of God and before he could move into the disposition of God, heaven itself would take a hand and display to all the touch of the Master. Silas and all in the assembly were about to witness "The Event!"

CHAPTER FIVE
THE EVENT

Silas was working down through his sermon outline. He was about twelve minutes into a planned thirty-five to forty minute lesson. He had just finished page four and was moving to the part of the lesson where he would talk about the various dispositions of God.

Milton was sitting on the last pew next to the aisle. Each row slowly dropped toward the pulpit, like in a movie theatre, so one could see over the head of those in front. While Milton was enjoying gazing around at the people, he wondered if it might not be about time to "sneak out" since the singing was over and the sermon did not seem promising.

Emma had decided it was time for her weekly exit. For several minutes she displayed her usual squirming and fidgeting, and when she thought the time was right, whispered into her mother's ear the need to go to the bathroom. Nancy had whispered back, "Oh, no you don't!"

Emma waited for the appropriate lapse of time and then, while showing grim discomfort on her face, Emma declared, "I really, really gotta go or burst!"

As was always the case, Emma got her way. Nancy slowly

stepped into the aisle and helped Emma navigate out of the pew. Then Nancy braced Emma as they began the walk up the aisle to the back of the auditorium.

Milton, having grown bored with people gazing and listening to the minister's homily, was just about to leave when he saw Nancy step from her pew. Then he saw Emma step into the aisle.

As Nancy helped Emma slowly struggle up the aisle, Milton was filled with compassion. Emma, as she took each step, displayed a smile that demanded a response, and Milton felt himself smiling back at her. As Nancy worked to help Emma, Milton knew that somehow he needed to help.

Without thinking, Milton arose from his pew, with thoughts rushing through his mind. "Maybe I can help the child with an operation; maybe I can just help the child up the aisle."

As Milton stepped into the aisle, something passed through his body like an electrical charge. Suddenly it seemed that he and everyone around him were moving in slow motion. Then a clear voice spoke to Milton's heart, "Tell Emma, Jesus the Christ heals you!"

Milton was staggered. He was trying to figure out what he was doing in the aisle and how he might help, but again the voice declared, "Tell Emma, Jesus the Christ heals you!"

As Nancy struggled with Emma, they approached Milton who was now standing in the middle of the aisle. As Emma drew near, Milton, without even realizing it, squatted to the floor and reached his arms out to her. All the onlookers thought the stranger was simply going to lift Emma and help her and her mother to the back.

Emma rolled into Milton's arms but instead of lifting her, he drew her in and whispered into her ear, "Emma, Jesus the Christ heals you!"

Milton's words startled Emma and she jerked backward. Her backward plunge threw Nancy's balance off and she began to fall backward, pulling Emma with her.

To the gasp of onlookers, both Nancy and Emma fell backward on the sloping floor. Nancy landed hard on her buttocks with Emma ending up between her legs.

As people began to pour into the aisle to help them, the commotion brought Silas' sermon to a halt. Everyone's focus was on Emma and her mom.

As Milton was trying to stand up, the folks entering the aisle just passed him aside as they rushed to have a part in the resurrection of Nancy and Emma. Milton, who was totally embarrassed by events, headed out the door, got into his pickup, and drove away and wondered what in the world had come over him.

Back in the church auditorium, all attention had been passed to Nancy and Emma as a cortege of people assisted them out of the auditorium and into the foyer where an inordinate amount of attention was bestowed upon them. Truth is, neither Nancy nor Emma had been hurt by the event, but attention was always welcomed.

Silas knew his time in the pulpit was over; his last sermon would never be finished. He announced, "Be assured, everyone is alright, but we have had enough excitement." He directed the song leader to close the service with a song and prayer as he slowly slipped down from the pulpit for the last time.

Words of comfort and conversations continued in the foyer. While Nancy and Emma were still the center of attention, several of the ladies were hunting for someone to blame for the ruckus. Before long, everyone agreed that the stranger who knelt in the aisle was the cause of the accident. As one lady said, "Everyone knows Emma goes up that aisle every week. If that stranger had just stayed out of the way, everything would have been fine."

Emma, several times, tried to tell her mother what the stranger had whispered in her ear, but each time Emma's mother would brush aside her words by saying, "Yes, Emma. We all pray that someday God will help you walk."

Soon everyone had expressed an appropriate amount of concern, and the people began to slowly fade and go home. Even Silas paid homage and expressed hope and goodwill for both Nancy and Emma. Then, like everyone else, Nancy, Nora, and Emma went home for Sunday lunch.

After eating lunch, Emma, as was her habit on Sunday afternoon, told her mother that she would like to lie down for a while. Nora told Nancy not to get up from her chair and that she would help Emma out of her braces, and the two headed down the hall to Emma's bedroom.

Unlacing the braces always provided a pleasant feeling to Emma, and Nora was pleased to see her roll on to her bed with less struggle than usual. With a rub of her hand over Emma's forehead, Nora bid her to have a good rest and gave her a parting nudge.

As Emma settled in, Nora joined Nancy in the living room where they would share the Sunday paper until one or both fell asleep.

Maybe a half hour had passed when Emma was suddenly

awakened. She had an immediate need to go to the bathroom. Without even thinking, she sprang from the bed and headed down the hall. She was more than half way to the bathroom when she realized that she was not wearing her braces. Emma let out a cry of surprise that woke both Nancy and Nora, and as they both reached the hall, there was Emma standing by the bathroom. "Dear God!" cried Nancy, "Emma, you can walk!"

CHAPTER SIX
THE APPRAISAL

Emma could walk! Nancy's, Nora's, and Emma's joy were beyond control. Emma could walk without braces! Soon laughs, cheers and tears filled the house as they danced and skipped through every room in the small frame house called home. Then all of a sudden a thought hit Nancy. What if all this gayety is not good for Emma? What if her walking is only temporary?

"Emma, Emma, you should settle down; you must be careful," Nancy declared as she took Emma's hand and led her to a nearby chair.

Though Emma could not understand her mother's reservation, she could tell by the tone of her voice that compliance was mandatory. "What's wrong, mother?" Emma asked. "Isn't it all just too wonderful? Isn't it all a miracle?"

Of course it was wonderful and maybe a miracle, but Nancy's concern had now infected Nora and both felt it best for Emma to take things easy until she could be carefully examined by the doctors. There would be time for jubilation later. However, while the doctors would have to wait until Monday, both ladies decided that a telephone call to the deacons and Silas would be appropriate.

A couple of telephone calls were made and the small community's communication tree went to work. Shortly, nearly all the church folks and most of the citizens of Eatton were aware of Emma's good fortune. Before long, hoards of people were stopping by in hopes that they could see Emma walk. Each new group of visitors initiated a repeat of the day's events.

Upon hearing the story of Emma's spontaneous recovery, a few declared the event a miracle, some attributed the outcome to a serendipitous result of Nancy's and Emma's fall, but all considered the event astonishing.

Over the next few days, between doctor appointments, the local community paper interviewed, took pictures, and ran Emma's story in the weekly Gazette.

When the doctors' reports started coming in, a more pragmatic reason for Emma's recovery was presented. The doctors had previously believed that Emma's accident had caused the severing of many of the nerves in her spinal column that controlled her legs. As a result, the prognosis was that her inability to walk was irreversible.

Obviously the present situation required a review of the earlier findings, and after the review it was concluded that the initial accident had but severely pinched and damaged the nerves instead of severing them. Emma's fall must have caused an adjustment of the spinal cord that resulted in a release of the nerves. The pious physicians even concluded that in all probability, Emma had been improving all along and the fall in the church simply accelerated her recovery.

As the days and weeks passed, the event was slowly forgotten.

CHAPTER SEVEN
AFTERMATH: SILAS

A few weeks after Silas ceased working with the congregation in Eatton, he was offered a job with Humpton Funeral Home. His new job would take him to Burville, a town of about twelve thousand people located some twenty three miles south from Eatton.

Silas' new job provided him with an apartment over the garage where the funeral home's hearse was parked. He was expected to assist the driver in picking up the deceased whenever called, and he was to comfort the bereaved. However, in comforting, he was instructed to speak very little; his employer told him, "Just be there to provide assurance that we care and will take good care of their loved one."

As the weeks and months slipped by, Silas began to enjoy his work. He learned that comforting others was more a matter of presence than words, and that a slight smile showing understanding or lightly touching one's hand spoke volumes.

As Silas learned the value of silence, his enjoyment of comforting people developed into a love for the work. One day, at the gravesite of a child whose family he had helped, he was approached by the mother of the deceased child. "Silas," she said, "we would have never made it through this tragedy without your kindness. We were not surprised to learn from Mr. Humpton that you are a minister. Thank you, Silas, for truly ministering to us."

As the people and family faded from the cemetery, Silas found a private place and began to weep uncontrollably. He realized that he was happy, and, after forty years, he had found his ministry.

CHAPTER EIGHT
AFTERMATH: MILTON

When Milton pulled out of the parking lot of the Eatton church following "the event," he knew that the more miles he could put between himself and Eatton the better he would feel. He could not understand or explain what had come over him. Milton was in agony, "What is wrong with me; what in the world came over me; have I gone crazy; why did I tell that child that God would heal her; how will she feel when she wakes up in the morning, still a cripple?"

As Milton continued to travel down the road, he contemplated the audacious comments made to the child, and slowly became equally puzzled by the inner voice that drove him to his bazaar behavior. "What force compelled me to do what I did?" thought Milton. "Who entered my mind? Have I gone mad?"

As he drove, the rhythmic sounds produced by the truck as it bounced along the highway slowly brought relief to his anxiety. Chip, who had sensed Milton's stress, decided it was time to give his master a lick of affection and bury his head in Milton's side. Chip's act did not go unnoticed. It brought Milton back to reality, and he realized that he was entering Guton, a small fishing community on the Colorado River some six miles north of Burville.

Seeing the sign that pointed to the lodge Milton had planned to visit, he slowed and turned in. "Chip," he said, "we planned on fishing here for a few days; let's not let a little temporary craziness stop us!"

The next few days were fun and relaxing for both Milton and Chip. Fishing was good and they made friends with the early risers who daily visited Mable's River Front Café. After a few days, he had nearly forgotten the events of the previous Sunday.

It was Thursday afternoon. Milton and Chip had spent the morning fishing in the rain. They could have done without the rain, but the fishing had been great. Shortly after noon, the sun broke through the clouds, which was a welcome sight, but the sun also changed fishing conditions and the fish just quit biting.

After putting away his fishing gear and feeding Chip, Milton headed for the Café. The lunch crew had already gone and the Café was empty except for Mable and a couple of old timers seated over in a corner. As Milton came through the door, Mable, who had been discussing the news with the old timers, turned with a look of acknowledgement and encouraged him to, "Come on over and help us with this problem."

As Milton headed for the corner to join the others he started talking from across the room, "What world problems are you trying to solve today? Mable, I need a big bowl of your stew and a glass of tea."

Mable waved an acknowledgment and headed for the kitchen as one of the old timers began to speak to Milton. "It's an article in the Eatton Gazette that has us in a puzzlement," the old timer snorted. "Seems they are reporting a story about a crippled girl, named Emma, who was healed last Sunday in church."

Milton grabbed the paper and started reading. As he absorbed the story he felt his body growing hot, then limp. His eyes filled with tears and he knew he had to get out, he needed air.

"It's true! It's all true!" Milton cried, as he bolted from the Café and scrambled for the safety of his room in the lodge.

For the next few hours, Milton was in turmoil. He prayed and he cussed, he cried and he laughed, "What does it all mean, God? What do you want?" While no answers came immediately, time did allow him to develop perspective. "There is no doubt; what is, is; the girl can walk." He continued, "The voice I heard was real; I'm not crazy."

Milton slowly calmed and began to feel good about what had happened, and he began to feel good about his involvement. "I don't understand; why me, God, but I am so grateful for the ride."

By morning Milton was resolved, "If this is how you plan to use me, I am ready! From this day on, Chip and I will travel the land doing good wherever you say."

Friday was a busy day for Milton. Most of the day was spent on the telephone and in the lodge's office faxing information to lawyers, banks, and his businesses. He was committed to his new found ministry, and he was divesting himself of all business matters that might hinder his new perspective.

Milton was a happy man Saturday morning as he visited the Café for the last time. He would eat, he and Chip would fish one last time, and then he would pack up to continue his journey to points unknown. Well, not totally unknown.

Milton had decided that Sunday morning he would travel the seventeen miles north to Eatton. He would visit the church in order to give Emma a big hug; he wanted to see her walk and confirm to himself God's great miracle.

After bidding goodbye to Mable and the old timers, Milton and Chip headed to the river. It was cloudy and raining again. The earlier rains had filled the river to the banks and quickened the current. Fishing would be good if one kept his hook under the rip current.

Milton was telling Chip that it was time to "throw the last hook," when he heard hollering coming from across the river and upstream. A man and woman were waving their arms frantically and screaming. As Milton tried to decipher their sounds and body language, his eyes caught glimpses of a child bobbing up and down in the swift moving current of the river. Without a second thought, he plunged into the river after the boy; Chip followed Milton.

The Sunday edition of the Burville News carried the story, "Man and His Dog Drown Saving Child."

CHAPTER NINE
AFTERMATH: EMMA

Emma could walk. She went to church on the very Sunday evening she first walked. To the delight of all, Emma walked, whirled, and jumped. Everyone rejoiced and called it a miracle.

In the days that followed, she was poked and prodded by physicians as they developed their theories about her unusual recovery. By the end of the week, everyone had an opinion and it was about fifty-fifty: either a miracle or spinal cord recovery. Emma didn't know what to think. She was eleven years old and just happy to be walking.

To her delight, when public school started, Emma enrolled. Though she was small and petite, she was bright and soon merged in with the other girls. At first, she often thought about the day of the event and wondered about its meaning or purpose. But with the passage of time, and with the activities of school and friends to run around with, she soon forgot to think about the event.

The months and years took wing and Emma grew into womanhood. Soon it was time for her to graduate from high school and on the last day of school she would also celebrate her eighteenth birthday. She had hoped to go to college, but her mother and grandmother could not afford to send her and there were no scholarships available. She was resolved to go to work.

It was on the very afternoon Emma was dressing for graduation that they heard someone knocking on the door. As Nora opened the door, a well-dressed, kindly looking gentleman asked, "Is this the home of Emma Harrison?" When Nora replied that it was, he continued, "My name is Gerald Hawkins. I am an attorney with Baker, Givens and Hawkins; I have business with Miss Emma Harrison; may I come in?"

After Emma, Nora, Nancy, and Mr. Hawkins were seated, Mr. Hawkins began. "Just before his death seven years ago, Mr. Milton Webb, inventor of the G-P-L valve, set money aside for the creation of the Emma Harrison Education, Development, and Welfare Foundation. The Foundation was to be turned over to you, Emma, on your eighteenth birthday. That's today. My firm was retained for an additional ten years to assist you in whatever ways you might need. The Foundation is sizable, in excess of two hundred million dollars. In addition, I have been instructed to personally deliver this sealed envelope from Mr. Milton Webb to you, Miss Emma Harrison."

Emma took the envelope and retreated to her room. While she could hardly take in all that had been said, she opened the envelope and read:

Dear Emma:

I am the man who told you that Jesus the Christ heals you. In hind sight, that day was more for me than you. That day I did not know enough to believe; now I do.

Through you, God gave me everything I could ever want or need. Really, I did nothing that day. It was all a gift from

God. Now, on this, your eighteenth birthday, I want to give you a gift that is just from me to you.

When I learned the truth about your healing, I set up a blind trust that would mature on your eighteenth birthday. I have no idea what its value will be when you receive it, but I have retained attorneys who will continue to look after the trust until you get whatever education you need to manage the Foundation yourself.

Old Chip, my dog, and I are probably still bouncing around the back country doing what little we can. I leave it up to you, Emma, to use the Foundation to the glory of God.

Sincerely, Milton

CHAPTER TEN
AS YOU WANT

The story is told of an old wise man that lived in a community. He often gave advice to parents that irritated the children. He would say such things as, "Children should be in submission to their parents and teachers; children should do their homework; children should not stay out late at night; children should be respectful of others and property..."

The children of the community decided that life would be much better if the old wise man could, somehow, be discredited. After many planning sessions the children came up with a plan that was sure to work.

The children would capture a live bird. One of the children would hold the bird cupped in his hands behind his back. Another child would ring the doorbell of the old man's house. When the old man answered the door, the boy with the bird would ask, "Tell me, old man, what have I behind my back?" When the old man heard the bird chirping, he would say, "You have a bird." Now the trap was set. When the old man acknowledged the bird, the boy would say, "Yes, now tell me old man is the bird dead or alive?"

If the old man said the bird was alive, the boy would squeeze the life out of the bird and present the bird saying,

"You are a fool old man; see, the bird is dead!" On the other hand, if the old man anticipated the action of the boy and said, "The bird is dead," the boy would deliver the live bird and say, "You are a fool old man; see, the bird is alive!"

Believing they had a fool proof plan, the boys caught their bird and proceeded to the old man's house. Upon arrival they knocked on his door. After a short wait, the door slowly opened and the old man carefully viewed the boys standing at his door. "How may I help you boys today?" the old man asked as he smiled.

The boy with the bird behind his back stepped up. "Tell me, if you can, what have I behind my back?"

The old man listened for a moment and then said softly, "Why, boys, you have a bird."

"Yes, Yes!" the boy responded, "But tell me, is the bird dead or alive?"

The old man paused and looked deeply into the eyes of the boys. With a smile he replied, "Boys, that bird is as you want!"

Indeed, the story of Silas, Milton, and Emma must be viewed from the perspective: "as you want".

Perhaps Silas was the victim of undue social pressure when he was but a boy. Perhaps his Aunt Ammoreta and the others in the church would have served Silas better had they suggested he go to mortuary school. Perhaps Silas' life is an example of one simply choosing a career that does not fit his disposition.

Perhaps Milton was simply the victim of emotional exuberance. Perhaps he wanted his life to have greater meaning and the cripple child just happened to be at the right place and time to plunge him into a wish fulfilling emotional fantasy.

Perhaps Emma's backward fall at church simply resulted in a serendipitous outcome. Perhaps she was but one of many medical examples reported annually where the patient spontaneously recovers from a presumed chronic condition. Perhaps... ... ...

On the other hand, perhaps the lives of Silas, Milton, and Emma are but examples of God's mysterious providence. Perhaps God does intertwine the lives of people as he choreographs the secrets of heaven's tapestry. Perhaps, God is God.

THE END

THE SPHERE

CHAPTER ONE
THE PRESENTATION

He was a small old man, no more than five feet four and couldn't have weighed more than a hundred and forty pounds. His dark suit and white shirt needed pressing; his tie was wrinkled and faded. His eye glasses sat on the end of his nose and his white hair was windblown; his socks were white and his shoes were scuffed. However, as he addressed the receptionist at the Pentagon's information desk, his voice was strong and clear. "Miss, my name is John Mills. I would like to speak to someone in authority who works in research and development. I have a discovery that is of the upmost importance."

Marge, the receptionist, was not unfamiliar with kooks who would bring their inventions or ideas to the Pentagon seeking an audience. There was a procedure. "Mr. Mills, will you please take a seat," pointing across the corridor to a wooden bench, "and I will find someone who can help you."

As the old man headed to the bench, Marge placed a call to security to report the need for assistance, and perhaps to talk with Lieutenant Jack Stoner with whom she had a date just the night before. However, the office secretary took the call, and after being assured that the call was not an emergency, informed Marge that someone would come her way when possible.

The morning passed, and as Marge was returning from lunch she noticed Mr. Mills was still sitting on the bench. Another call to security yielded the same response, "we will have someone help you as soon as possible."

It was a little after four in the afternoon when Marge realized that Mr. Mills was still waiting and no one had come to help. This time Marge opened her cell phone and called Lieutenant Stoner directly. When she was instructed to leave a message, she said, "Jack, I need your help. Please come to my desk as soon as you can."

It was four-thirty when Lieutenant Stoner strolled up to the information desk. "Hi, Marge."

"Jack, that man has been patiently waiting all day to talk with someone," pointing across the corridor. "He seems like a sweet old guy. I want you to go talk with him."

With a little more information and assuring Marge that he would be right back, Jack moved across the corridor toward John Mills.

"Mr. Mills, I am Lieutenant Stoner. I understand you have something you would like to share with us."

As Lieutenant Stoner was talking, John Mills opened a sack that had all the appearances of a lunch bag and pulled out a silver sphere that was about four inches in diameter.

"Lieutenant," John said, "I must go; I have a plane to catch. You must take this sphere to the authorities in research and development. Show it to them and if they are interested have them contact me." As he was speaking, he placed the sphere in Lieutenant Stoner's hand.

"Wait! What do I tell them? What are they supposed to do with it? How do we reach you? I need more information."

"Lieutenant, I am Doctor John Mills. I am a professor at Whorton Christian College in Doby, Texas. Get the sphere to research and tell them to watch it. You know how to reach me if they are interested."

As he finished talking, Professor Mills shook Lieutenant Stoner's hand and proceeded to the door. The Pentagon's speaker system had already announced that it was closing to the public and guards were gathering at the exit to assist visitors leaving the building.

Lieutenant Stoner stood bewildered; he was holding a sphere about the size of a cannon ball that was supposed to do something, and the old professor who gave it to him was gone. He shook his head and wondered, "What do I do with this ball now?"

Jack returned to Marge's desk as she was gathering up her belongings to go home. "Thanks, Jack. I owe you."

"I'll say. You owe me big! Look, the old man gave me a cannon ball and wants us to watch it!"

"What's it supposed to do?" Marge inquired as she lifted her purse and started for the exit door.

"I don't know. I'll take it to the security office and leave it with Major Reno till tomorrow. Wait for me and I will walk you out."

As Lieutenant Stoner entered the security office, the shift was changing, and the skeleton night crew was gathering around the security monitors. Major Reno, Chief of Security, had already left, and his secretary was about to walk out the door.

Lieutenant Stoner spoke to Major Reno's secretary. "Before you leave I need to store this ball in the major's office."

The secretary glanced at the ball. "What on earth is that? What's it for?"

"I don't know," the Lieutenant sighed. "Just put it on his desk, and I'll talk to him about it in the morning."

The secretary grudgingly took the ball and gently placed it on the major's desk and both the secretary and Lieutenant Stoner left for the night.

CHAPTER TWO
THE SPHERE

Lieutenant Stoner had just arrived at work the following morning when Major Reno's secretary stepped into his office. "Lieutenant Stoner, Major Reno needs to see you ASAP."

As he entered the major's office, Major Reno pointed to the silver sphere sitting on his desk. "Jack, what is that?"

Lieutenant Stoner proceeded to explain the circumstances of the sphere but was interrupted by Major Reno. "Jack, move it off my desk! Just try to move it!"

Lieutenant Stoner walked over to the desk to pick up the sphere. As he wrapped his hand around it and tried to lift it off the desk, he realized that he could not pick it up. Quickly stabilizing his footing, the lieutenant cupped both hands around the sphere and pulled with all his might. Nothing! It was as if the sphere was glued to the desk.

"Jack, is this some kind of joke?" Major Reno growled. "Have you glued a cannon ball to my desk top? This isn't funny!"

Lieutenant Stoner assured the major that he had done nothing with the sphere, and that he had not placed it on the major's desk. As they continued to talk, they were interrupted by the sound of a soft thud to the floor. Looking down, both men were startled to see that the silver sphere had rolled off the desk and was resting on the floor.

Lieutenant Stoner reached down and picked up the sphere. It was no heavier than a tennis ball. As shock gave way to curiosity, he and Major Reno passed the sphere back and forth as they discussed what to do next. Finally, Major Reno instructed him to take the sphere to the lab located in the basement of the Pentagon. "Lieutenant, we will let the nerds figure this one out."

As Lieutenant Stoner headed out the door of the security offices, located on the third floor of corridor three, he realized that the lab, located in the basement, would not open for another forty-five minutes. Since it was on his way, he had time to call Marge and have her meet him at the Ground Zero Café in the Pentagon's courtyard.

Ten minutes later, Jack and Marge were enjoying a cup of coffee and discussing the professor and the sphere. "Let me see it again, Jack," Marge begged. As Jack handed it to her the sphere seemed to be light as a feather. In fact, as she reached for the sphere, its unexpected weightlessness caused it to slip off her fingers and slowly float across the table. Marge and Jack looked at each other in amazement as the sphere bounced, then floated above the table top, and began rising upward like a helium balloon.

Jack reached for the sphere, but it had cleared his fingertips and continued to rise. He grabbed a chair to stand on, but by then the sphere had risen above the second floor and was gaining speed. They stared upward watching the sphere until it vanished from sight.

Jack looked at Marge. "What will I tell the major? I've lost the sphere!"

Marge went with Jack to the security office to support his story, but the major was not in an understanding mood. "You what? You lost the sphere? It floated away? I'm supposed to believe that a ball that neither of us could lift became lighter than air? Lieutenant, have you lost your mind?"

It took some effort, but after hearing the story from the lieutenant, Marge, and several officers who were also at the café, the major became convinced that the sphere had indeed taken flight. The question remaining was, "what do we do now?"

Lieutenant Stoner suggested that they contact Professor Mills, tell him what had happened and ask if he had a duplicate. Major Reno replied, "Sure, call the Professor and tell him we lost his sphere. I don't think so. The Professor knew very well what the sphere would do. In fact, he is probably behind its disappearance."

After instructing Lieutenant Stoner and Marge to keep quiet about all the events surrounding the sphere, he informed them that he would take the matter up with General Cheran who was in charge of military intelligence and had offices in the Pentagon. Later in the day Major Reno met with the general.

"General, I need to report an incident. Yesterday a professor from a small college in Texas presented a sphere to one of our security officers. His only instructions were to 'watch the sphere and see what it would do.' The weight of the sphere was strangely unstable. Then suddenly, I assume on a preprogrammed command, the sphere became lighter than air, escaped our custody, and disappeared into the atmosphere. The actions of the sphere are of national interest, and I believe we should learn more about its origin and technology."

General Cheran was fascinated with the potential of the sphere, if it really could do what had been described, and authorized Major Reno to take whatever steps necessary to ascertain the origin and technology of the sphere. Also, the general assigned three experienced field agents to assist the major. The mission was classified as top secret in the interest of national security. The major was to file a complete report in ten days.

Major Reno was delighted with the assignment. He wanted to be in military intelligence, and this assignment would be his entry ticket. When he returned to his office, the major was thinking about the meeting he would have with his field agents the next morning. He was surprised to see Lieutenant Stoner waiting for him, and he invited the lieutenant to follow him into his office. As the major browsed through the materials left on his desk, the lieutenant spoke. "Major, I've been waiting for you. I want to be a part of the team that will look into the sphere."

"Not possible, Lieutenant. You don't have the field experience necessary for the job."

"But, Major, I'm the only one, excluding the receptionist, who has seen Professor Mills."

The major slid a photo that had been lying on his desk across to the lieutenant. "Isn't that our man?"

"Yes, Sir, but…"

The major interrupted, "Lieutenant, it wasn't hard to find Professor Mills. He teaches music and art appreciation to freshmen at a small college in Texas. He has a bachelor, master and doctor degrees in fine arts. He knows nothing about science or technology. He is not our target. He is fronting for someone else. He is only the key to the target. Thank you for your interest and offer, but this mission is for the intel professionals."

CHAPTER THREE
THE MISSION

It was early morning when Major Reno entered the security offices. However, three men in civilian clothing were already waiting for him. As he opened the door to his office, the men followed and one spoke, "Major, General Cheran sent us. We have been assigned to help you with a little problem. The General suggested we dress in civilian clothing."

The major was new to intelligence work, but was excited about the mission. "Tell me about yourselves."

"I'm Master Sergeant Edward Backus, team leader. I specialize in electronics."

"Sergeant Grant Warren, sir. I specialize in weapons and explosives."

"Sir, I'm Corporal William Hunter. I'm a medic and specialize in interrogation drugs."

The major was impressed with the men and was anxious to get the mission underway. After briefing them on the sphere and events, he was ready to define the mission. "The mission will be in three parts: One—Who is the person or persons responsible for the technology; Two—Is the sphere a hoax or is it a new technology; Three—If the technology is real, we are to take custody of it."

Backus surmised, "Then you want us to go to Texas and squeeze information from Mills?"

"No," the major replied. "As I said, Professor Mills is undoubtedly a front man, and you only send a decoy when you seek to keep the original a secret. We must assume, until proven otherwise, that the technology is real and that it has been or will be offered to other governments also. I suspect that the source behind the technology is looking for the highest bidder. I want to go in quietly and find the source before anyone knows we are in town. We do not want to scare off the source and lose the technology. I will remain in D.C. where I can quickly gather information on all suspects and cut through the red tape when necessary. You three will go to Doby, Texas, check into an out-of-the-way motel called Hunter's Lodge and start gathering intel. Put ears in Professor Mills' house, telephone, car, and office. Check on friends of Mills who also work at Whorton College. We will communicate daily or more often when necessary. Any questions?"

The three men nodded their heads affirming acknowledgment and rose to leave the room. The major walked them to the door and gave his final instructions. "Wheels up in two hours. You will be in Doby by fourteen hundred and set up by evening. Confirm your status by eighteen hundred hours."

CHAPTER FOUR
WORKING THE MISSION

The following three days and nights were busy and filled with frustration. Backus, Warren, and Hunter spent their nights searching offices, homes, garages, and cars for clues. During the day they listened to voice recordings hoping to hear someone drop a name or new lead.

Back in Washington, Major Reno checked the telephone records of more than seventy people in hopes of finding new information. Professor Mills, nearly all the professors at Whorton, and the records of many associates located at other schools were checked for clues. Not one name surfaced that could link the person to the technology.

By the sixth day, stress and frustration were apparent when Master Sergeant Backus and Major Reno had their nightly discussion.

"Major, we've searched this whole town and listened to hours of chatter. I can tell you all the nasty gossip on everyone, but I can't provide you with one clue that gets us closer to the target."

"Backus, one of two things has happened, and I don't like either. Either they know we are here and have gone silent or they've moved on, and Mills is out of the loop. I'm afraid the longer we wait the less Mills can tell us. It's time we play hard ball. We need Mills to talk and we need it now."

"Major, am I to understand that you are giving us a green light to take whatever action is necessary to extract from Mills information relative to the technology and personnel associated with the sphere?"

"Sergeant, you have read me correctly, and I want that information within three days. I am to report to the General four days from now. Get me something."

"I understand, Major. We will not disappoint the General."

Backus hung up the telephone and joined Warren and Hunter who were listening to the telephone chatter recently recorded. "Anything?" Backus asked as he entered the room.

"No," smiled Warren, "except Mr. Logan is hiding Mrs. Murphy's newspapers because of her cat's nightly screeching."

"Well put it all away, gentlemen. We are through listening and searching. The major is running out of time. He has given us the green light to crack Mills. Tomorrow is Friday, and we will sack him and take him out of his world. Then we have until Sunday night to confine, isolate, break, and extract the information we need. Monday morning he'll wake up in his own bed with nothing but nightmares. Hunter, how's the timing with the drugs?"

"I'd like three days, but two will do. We'll just fancy up the cocktail."

Master Sergeant Backus pulled up a chair and laid out the plan. "Late tomorrow night we will sack the subject. We will bind, blind, and confine Mills with tape so he cannot move or talk, and take him to the old vacant farm house we found. We will tape him to the chair and isolate him for twenty-four hours. No talking, no sounds. Then we will give him some water, properly drugged, and start the interrogation with additional cocktails as needed. By Sunday afternoon, he should be spilling his guts and all his secrets. When we get what we want, we flush him out and take him home. Does this sound okay to you guys?"

Both Warren and Hunter nodded in agreement and Backus ended the meeting. "Take the night off guys, and sleep in late. Tomorrow night is game time."

CHAPTER FIVE
THE SECRET

It was two-fifteen in the morning when Backus, Warren, and Hunter entered John Mills' house. The capture went without incident. With a sack over Mills' head, his legs and arms bound, and mouth covered with cloth and tape, he was easily transported to the farm house as planned.

By three-thirty, John Mills was taped to a chair and except for a moan from time to time, silence filled the house. Quietly, Backus, Warren, and Hunter took turns guarding the subject as the clock ticked away.

At first, Mills struggled with his confinement. He would stiffen his body and try to stand, but the tape held firm. He would try to rock the chair, but it was nailed to the floor, and as the hours passed Mills seemed to become resolved to his predicament and became passive. However, just before lunch on Sunday, Mills stirred again and became agitated. He struggled, jerked, and rocked for several minutes and then slumped over and went limp.

Hunter had been watching Mills when he began to struggle and noticed with concern when he went limp. Hunter, against rules, reached down and felt Mills' pulse. He couldn't find it.

"Backus, Warren, get in here. We have a problem."

By the time Backus and Warren entered the room, Hunter had cut Mills' tape and had laid him on the floor.

"What are you doing? He's in isolation," roared Backus.

"Forget isolation. Mills has had a heart attack. I can hardly feel a pulse. We've got to get him to a doctor, and quick!"

Backus paused, "Wait a minute. Let's think ... yes, let's get him to the doctor. We can't let him die until we get the information. Get the tape off, and we'll drive him to the hospital and tell them our friend is having a heart attack."

On the way to the hospital, Backus called Major Reno.

"We've had a setback, Major. John Mills has had a heart attack. He hasn't told us anything yet. We are in route to the hospital now."

"Keep Mills alive, Backus," replied Reno. "He's the only one who can tell us anything. Keep me informed."

The doctors were with John Mills for several hours working to keep him alive. Finally one of the doctors entered the waiting room and reported, "Gentlemen, Mr. Mills has had a massive heart attack. He is alive, but I doubt that he will make it through the day. There is too much damage."

"Can he talk?" Backus inquired. "Can we talk with him? It is very important that we talk with him."

"I'm sorry," replied the doctor. "He awakens for a few seconds from time to time and mumbles a few words, but he's too sick to have visitors or carry on a conversation."

Backus made another call to Major Reno. "It doesn't look good. Mills is dying. He comes to from time to time, but the doctors won't let us see him."

"Sergeant, you've got to get in there and ask Mills who made the sphere. We must know about the sphere."

Backus assured the major that he would try, but he knew time was running out. Then Backus had a thought. He noticed an orderly was regularly going in and out of Mills' room. All he needed was an orderly's coat and a distraction.

A few minutes later, Backus had found an orderly's coat and had instructed Warren and Hunter to distract Mills' orderly the next time he left the room.

When the room was clear, Backus entered Mills' room. "Mr. Mills, can you hear me?"

Mills stirred and slowly opened his eyes.

"Mr. Mills, tell me who made the sphere?"

"What? Who made what? The sphere?"

"Yes, who made the sphere?"

"The sphere? It's a girl's shot put. It has no value."

"Mr. Mills, the sphere could fly. How, how does it work? Who works it?"

"I did."

"What? How did you work it?"

"I wanted to share with others what I had learned. I learned to control the sphere with my mind!"

With those words Professor John Mills drifted off into a coma and died twenty minutes later.

THE END

SOVIET 7

CHAPTER ONE
INTRODUCTION

It was 1988, and Jesse Webb had a new job as assistant professor of computer technology at Brumton University. Only a few months earlier he had completed his dissertation for the doctor of philosophy in artificial intelligence and computer signatures. Specifically, Jesse had developed a frequency logarithm that would, theoretically, break signature entry codes and allow access into military grade satellites. In simple terms, Jesse had specialized in hacking into sophisticated computer systems.

Like the question of which came first, the chicken or egg, one might ask which drove the other: rocket science or computer science? Did computers solve the technology problems in rocket development or did the technology needed for rockets drive computer development? Whichever you choose, Jesse Webb was a product of the time.

In the late 1950s and sixties, rocket development was the central focus of the space program: the object was to "just get the thing off the ground." By the late sixties and seventies, the emphasis had shifted to payload; by the eighties, satellite security and spy satellites had become the rage. Dr. Jesse Webb had a special interest in satellite signature coding and protocol.

No one was surprised when Dr. Webb was invited to participate in a seminar sponsored by the NRO (National Reconnaissance Office). The NRO develops and operates unique and innovative space reconnaissance systems and conducts intelligence related activities essential for U.S. National Security.

Dr. Webb had been invited to one of the strategic war gaming seminars periodically sponsored by the NRO. The game usually consisted of six to eight invited guests who spent a few days attempting to find and communicate with a target satellite. The first to find the satellite won bragging rights. Should one actually break the satellite's code and make it "burp" (provide feedback), that person's name was placed on the plaque of "Meritorious Distinction in Satellite Reconnaissance", but over the twenty year period of its existence, only eight honored names decorated the plaque.

It was late August and Jesse was excited. He had been a teaching assistant while he worked on his degree. Now, he had a full-time job as an assistant professor, and to top it all, had been invited to the prestigious gaming activities of the NRO. As he packed for the three day trip, his mind was filled with the challenge of teaching and the excitement of gaming.

CHAPTER TWO
THE GAME

The NRO operates ground stations around the world that collect and distribute intelligence gathered from satellites. Four times a year the strategic war gaming division of NRO sponsors satellite gaming exercises in an ongoing effort to stay abreast of new technologies and innovative methodologies that could be employed in finding and identifying satellites.

This exercise, being conducted in late August 1988, would be comprised of six visiting professors. Five had participated in the process before; Professor Jesse Webb was the youngest and the novice.

The exercise would be somewhat different from the norm. All the participants would be looking for the same thing: a new Russian satellite that had been launched a few days earlier. It was believed that the satellite was a weather satellite and geostationary, meaning over the equator and stationary with the earth. However, the exact location of the satellite had yet to be determined, and the focus of the exercise was to find the satellite and identify its symbol rate and frequency.

Each participant was given a folder providing longitude,

latitude, and angles to be viewed. Each participant was to search the quadrant assigned and listen for signals not already recorded by NRO intelligence.

Unknown by Jesse, the other participants had agreed to play the customary prank on the "new kid". They had intercepted his data folder and carefully increased the viewing angle by several degrees. They would let the novice search deep space in vain for the first day before breaking the news and getting their laughs. Then they would give him the correct coordinates and have him join the others in the search.

As the first day began, each participant went to his designated work station and began the task of setting his directional antenna, actually a disk, to the proper angular positions. By mid-morning all participants had begun the process of slowly rotating their search antenna along the axis looking for a unique signal. This process would be repeated several times with each sweep moving only slightly up or down, depending upon the search pattern, within the designated coordinates. Satellite finding is like looking for a needle in a haystack. One might find a new satellite in ten minutes or it might take ten months.

About four o'clock in the afternoon, Professor Roark from Winston College, let out a holler. "I've found it!" He cheered as he waved papers full of data in his hand.

Dr. Blar, NRO Director of the project, took the data from Professor Roark and gave it a preliminary review. "Looks good. I think Dr. Roark may have found the new bird. But, I suggest we not share the exact coordinates until tomorrow morning. Why don't the rest of you keep searching for the satellite until tomorrow? Maybe one of you will find and verify the location. In the meantime, Dr. Roark, come with me and we will check the data."

As the room grew silent, each man returned to his cubical to continue work; Jesse was envious. Deep down he had wanted to find the satellite first. Sure, it was a long shot, but he had hoped that he would be the first to hear the "bleep" of a new satellite. Truth be told, Jesse was losing confidence. He had listened all day and had not heard one signature. Not one!

As early evening approached and fatigue set in, each participant began to fade for the day. Mid-evening everyone was gone but Jesse. Jesse just couldn't give up until he heard at least one signal. "I will stay all night if I have to, but I will not quit until I hear a signal."

It was three-twelve in the morning, and Jesse was wavering between consciousness and sleep when he heard a faint "bleep" on his earphones. Adrenaline surged through his body; he stood straight up and strained to hear the sound that had broken the silence.

Yes, there it was. A signal was coming in strong and clear, so Jesse began recording the signal and gathering location coordinates. Next, he compared the satellite's identifiers with known satellites. The signature was new. He was sure he, too, had found the new Russian weather satellite. Happy at last, Jesse went to bed.

It didn't matter to him that he had only three hours of sleep. He was up and back in his work area by eight the following morning. As the last participant arrived, Director Blar asked, "Did anyone else find the new Russian satellite?"

No one spoke until Jesse announced, "I found it!" He walked over to Dr. Blar and handed him his data showing coordinates and signal data.

After reviewing Jesse's date, Dr. Blar smiled, "Jesse I'm

afraid you've been taken for a ride. Your cohorts gave you coordinates that were way outside the viewing range, and your signal is a jumble of frequencies suggesting an echo from several satellites. I'm afraid you found space debris that was bouncing signals. Jesse, you've been had!"

Jesse turned red as the room filled with laughter. He tried to be a good sport about the deception, but it was hard to smile. Deep down, he was sure that he had identified a clear signal, but for now he would swallow his pride and join the pack.

Coordinates for the newly found satellite were given to all participants, and soon everyone was looking at the new bird. Its signal was clear and crisp, and Jesse could tell by the sound that what he had heard and recorded earlier was very different from what he was hearing now.

Late in the day as everyone was getting ready to quit, the audio sound of the satellite suddenly changed. The sound was familiar to Jesse. "What's happening?" he asked as he strained to hear the pulsating sound.

Dr. Blar listened and responded. "The symbol rate and frequency of the satellite seems to be changing, but what is really happening is an audio distortion caused by the oscillation of frequencies as the satellite receives and sends data at the same time."

Jesse nearly gasped aloud. "What if what I heard and recorded was caused by the same distortion? What if I did find something? I need to take more readings."

Everyone had gone for the evening, everyone but Jesse. He settled in for the long listening night. This time, he would be ready with a full array of power detectors, identifiers, satellite spectrum views, and receivers. If he heard the signal this time, he would take laser, radar, and infrared signatures of the satellite. This time, he would be ready.

At three-twelve in the morning, Jesse again heard the signal; yes, it was different from the new Russian weather satellite. Jesse knew that he had found a new satellite, and for the next twelve minutes, he recorded everything he could about the satellite. By the time the signal stopped, he had the satellite mapped in space. "Speak or don't speak," smirked Jesse. "I've got you—whoever you are."

The following morning brought the last day of exercises, and Dr. Blar announced his pleasure with the group. "Thank you for your participation in this exercise, and thank you for finding and mapping the new Russian weather satellite. It is mapped as RWS234. For the rest of the day you may try to penetrate the code of one of our own satellites known as USWS-457. The 457 is an old weather satellite that is about to go silent. See if you can breach its code. The information on the screen includes its coordinates. Please turn in all your data to me by five as we must exit the building by five-thirty. I will see each of you before your departure. A letter of appreciation to you and your institution will be forthcoming. Again, thank you for your participation."

Jesse didn't care much about playing with the USWS-457. He was determined to spend his last day trying to breach the satellite he had named X-1. All day long Jesse ran his frequency logs against the satellite. About four in the afternoon, he was aroused to the sound of his computer. His frequency log had penetrated the satellite. "I'm in!" thought Jesse. "I have breached the code of someone's satellite— American or Russian."

Jesse realized it would be wise to close the door to the satellite and say nothing about the visit. He knew what he had done and decided not to share everything. As five in the afternoon arrived, Jesse gathered up his notes and placed them in his briefcase. He would give Dr. Blar only the data on the location of the satellite and its unique signature.

As Jesse left the NRO facility he felt somewhat exonerated. No, he had not found the target satellite, but he had found something. While Dr. Blar had said nice things about his efforts as he departed, he could tell the speech was routine and absent of meaningful substance. Jesse left hoping that his data, when reviewed, would help his image by showing that he had, indeed, found something.

CHAPTER THREE
DISCOVERY

A few days following the conclusion of the satellite detection exercises at the NRO facilities, Dr. Blar was discussing the findings with the NRO Intelligence Committee, which reviews all pertinent materials gathered on satellites that might be of national interest.

Dr. Blar continued his report. "In addition to finding the newest Russian weather satellite, labeled RWS234, I want to also report an anomaly discovered by Dr. Jesse Webb. At first glance, his audio data appeared to simply be echo transmissions from other satellites. However, in addition to providing audio data, Dr. Webb provided us with a fixed position of a new object in space. Perhaps it is debris and the signal is a fading transmitter. Whatever it is, I think we should take a look."

The committee agreed with Dr. Blar's suggestion and authorized him to take the matter to central control where a team of specialists would gather data and send information to the super computer, nicknamed Nora, which would analyze and formulate a "best guess" scenario.

Ten days later, the super computer delivered a probable conclusion for the data presented. The conclusion startled everyone at the NRO. The findings were reported by Dr. Blar to the committee.

"Gentlemen and ladies," Dr. Blar began. "Two years ago, the intelligence community intercepted communications that suggested the Russians had successfully launched a military grade offensive weapons satellite. We code named the satellite Soviet 7 because we knew of six previous attempts and all had failed. For weeks we searched for the satellite without success and ultimately concluded that the report was no more than a rumor. Well, perhaps we were wrong. According to Nora, Dr. Webb may have stumbled upon a satellite which he calls X-1 that serves as the key to Soviet 7.

The satellite Dr. Webb found was emitting a strange signal, but Nora filtered the signal and concluded that it was three signals being emitted by X-1. One signal, the strongest, was pointed to earth and seemed to be sending weather data. A weaker signal was being transmitted with telemetry data from another object. The last signal, which was even weaker, was found to be feedback from the antenna on X-1 that was pointed away from earth toward deep space.

Nora reports a high probability that Dr. Webb found a satellite that was posing as a weather satellite, but in reality it is a communications satellite serving as a relay to a deep space satellite. Nora concludes that there is a high probability that the deep space satellite is the missing Soviet 7."

Silence filled the room. Everyone was stunned by the news that Soviet 7 could be a reality. Until this moment, Soviet 7, the title reserved for an offensive weapons satellite, was no more than an unsubstantial rumor.

Nathan Howell, chairman of the Intelligence Committee and advisor to the President, broke the silence. "Dr. Blar, I'm not taking this to the President until we know for sure that Soviet 7 exists. If it is out there, find it! Focus all the rabbit ears on the problem. Get back to Dr. Webb and see if he knows anything more. Do whatever has to be done, but find that satellite and find it fast!"

The meeting adjourned, but the potential of the problem brought concern and tension to everyone. Dr. Blar returned to his office and immediately instructed his assistant, John Mounty, to place a call to Dr. Webb. "Tell Dr. Webb that I need to see him ASAP. Tell him we will have a ticket waiting for him at the airport on the next flight to Washington. I'll see him first thing in the morning."

CHAPTER FOUR
THE HUNT FOR SOVIET 7

When Dr. Blar arrived at his office the next morning, John Mounty was waiting. "Dr. Webb is in the waiting room and he's not happy."

Dr. Blar looked surprised. "Not happy? Didn't you tell him why we needed him?"

John continued, "I didn't know how much I could tell him. I just told him to come immediately. When he asked why, I said it was a matter of national security."

As Dr. Blar moved to the door he replied, "Well, we'll only tell him what we have to in order to see if he knows anything more than what we already have."

Dr. Blar opened the door and reached out his hand as he moved toward Dr. Webb. "Good morning, Dr. Webb. Thank you for coming. Please come into my office. We have a few questions to ask about the data you submitted following the exercises."

Dr. Webb immediately questioned, "Am I in trouble? I know the satellite I mapped was not the target. I've looked over the data and I suspect the satellite was not one of ours. I'm thinking it was Russian. Are they mad? Have I caused a problem?"

"No, no, no!" Dr. Blar responded. "Let me assure you, you are not in trouble. In fact, we are pleased. You found a Russian satellite that had not been mapped. We're very interested and were wondering if you had any additional information on the satellite that you could share?"

Wondering the real reason he was called to Washington, Jesse asked, "What are you not telling me? What are you looking for?"

Dr. Blar knew he had to let Jesse in on some of the findings. "Dr. Webb, the signature of the satellite you call X-1 was cluttered because it was three signals in one."

"Of course!" Dr. Webb exclaimed. "That would dismiss the presumption of echo. I was sure that there was nothing close enough to cause such distortions. That baby isn't a weather satellite at all. It's a spy satellite isn't it?"

Dr. Blar realized that Dr. Webb had correctly summed up the situation and knew that it was time to tell him everything. "Jesse, we have a problem. The satellite you found is communicating with earth and another satellite. The weaker signals are being distorted by a primary signal designed to sound like routine weather data. We need to know what the satellite is talking to in deep space."

There was a long silence as Jesse carefully looked at Dr. Blar and evaluated his comments. "Howard," Jesse said slowly, "I cannot tell you what it's talking to, but I can tell you where to look."

"You've got to be kidding," Dr. Blar said with excitement. "Are you saying you know the location of Soviet 7?"

"I'm not familiar with the term Soviet 7," Jesse replied, "but I can tell you the location of the satellite that X-1 is talking to."

Dr. Blar could no longer contain himself. "Jesse, we believe X-1 is talking to a Russian offensive weapons satellite dubbed Soviet 7. We believe it is in deep space and we want to find it, take pictures, and, if possible, destroy the threat. I need your help."

Dr. Webb was drawn to the common cause. "I will be glad to help, but now I must tell you a little secret. I penetrated the entry code of X-1. I can enter X-1 and send any signal you want to Soviet 7."

"Hmmm!" groaned Howard. "The Russians change those codes every week. It's been ten days since you penetrated X-1. Oh, had we just acted earlier. Now, it could take days, weeks, or forever to do it again."

Jesse smiled.

"You put in a back door!" Howard exclaimed. "You sneak. You have a back door into X-1!!"

"Yes," Jesse replied. "X-1 is mine. The Russians will never find all my keys. The only way to close my door would be to gut the software."

For the rest of the day, Howard and Jesse were inseparable. Jesse provided Howard with coordinates to Soviet 7, and the NRO staff went to work turning the satellite toward the target. Within a few hours, laser and microwave radar, and a half dozen imaging cameras were capturing everything in the target area. By morning Soviet 7 would be mapped and pictured.

However, two issues continued to plague Howard and Jesse. Jesse could penetrate X-1, but he did not have the code to Soviet 7. While X-1 had access to Soviet 7, the code was randomized upon each visit. Thus, the code to Soviet 7 could only be accessed by X-1. This issue presented an additional problem.

When the Russians, who obviously watched Soviet 7, realized it was not responding or acting according to protocol, they would shut down X-1 and access Soviet 7 utilizing other methods. After all, the satellite was theirs; they had the codes, and of course, they also had backdoors.

Jesse, Howard, and the NRO staff would have to come up with a methodology that would allow them to access Soviet 7 and take control before the Russians could respond. The window would only last a few seconds, and there would be no second chances.

CHAPTER FIVE
THE END TO SOVIET 7

It was October. There had been dozens of strategy sessions and several meetings with the NRO intelligence committee. Reconnaissance data, including pictures, clearly revealed the presence of a satellite with a platform holding three, maybe five, intercontinental missiles. The President had been informed of the findings and provided recommendations for a solution. After discussions with the National Security Council, the President had given the green light to "take out" Soviet 7. However, there was disagreement as to what "take out" meant. Some wanted to simply destroy Soviet 7, others wanted to take control and possession of the satellite.

Jesse, because of his knowledge of X-1's code tables, and because he had more experience with X-1 than anyone else, had been appointed director of the project. In Jesse's mind, the directive from the President was clear; the words "take out" meant eliminate Soviet 7. Equally clear to Jesse was the international agreement that "no offensive weapons" would be launched into space. Oh, Jesse knew that he did not have privilege to the secrets of either Russia or the United States. Perhaps there were other offensive weapons floating in space—perhaps. However, in Jesse's mind the matter was clear. "I will not contribute to the danger. If I can, I will kill Soviet 7."

The strategy for killing Soviet 7 was complicated and would have to be carefully timed. First, an electronics aircraft would be sent aloft with jamming equipment. At the designated time, the airplane would report a jamming exercise with a ship at sea. The exercise would be located in a position that would cut off the X-1's signal from a direct path to Russia's receivers. Hopefully, the Russians would see the exercise as routine. Perhaps they would do nothing until it was time to communicate with X-1. However, more likely the Russians would switch to a backup using large receivers located in Australia that could relay data back to agencies or companies who paid for the services.

A special project team was sent to Australia. The team would cause an electrical power outage in the grid of the satellite receivers at the designated time. While the satellite receiver system had power generators that would kick in immediately, there would be a ninety second delay in transmissions while the equipment rebooted.

During the ninety second window of silence, Jesse would have to access X-1's code, send instructions to Soviet 7 to fire the downward thrusters, shift all outer fuel to the downward tanks, and bury a virus in the software that would prevent any override of the command controlling the downward thruster. Lastly, the virus would erase all command data and code tables. In essence, the downward thrusters would burn until all the fuel was gone, and then the virus would perform a lobotomy by erasing any avenue for gaining control of the satellite. Soviet 7 would push away from earth in an ever expanding orbit into outer space. Eventually, it would be grabbed by the sun's gravity and burn up.

While it should not be said that the strategy worked perfectly, it did work. On October 14, 1988, Dr. Jesse Webb and his crew launched their software attack on X-1 and Soviet 7. While the jamming of communication signals worked, the Russians did pickup signals of the attack. The Russians tried to counter attack by stopping the thrusters, but they were too late. Even better, their attention on the thrusters allowed Jesse to complete the implant of the virus. Soon, the game was over. Both the Americans and the Russians watched and listened as Soviet 7 slowly faded away. Within ten hours after igniting the thruster, Soviet 7 faded into outer space.

CHAPTER SIX
AFTERMATH

No newspaper or television network ever made a report about the demise of the Soviet 7. The Russians never publically protested or admitted the loss of one of their satellites. In fact, neither the Americans nor the Russians have ever acknowledged the affair.

It is true that a letter of protest was received from the government of Australia concerning the conduct of several drunken American soldiers who had visited their Satellite Communications Center. It seems that one of the soldiers, while hiding behind two others, threw a master switch knocking out the power to the whole grid. While Australia had been repaid handsomely for the expenses incurred as a result of the power outage, they still felt that some kind of disciplinary action against the soldiers was warranted. Australian authorities were assured that appropriate action would be taken for such despicable conduct.

Dr. Jesse Webb never returned to teaching. Brumton University released Dr. Webb from his teaching duties and contract. Perhaps it should also be mentioned a few days later, Brumton University was awarded a rather substantial government grant for the development of their computer science programs.

It might also be noteworthy to remember that from 1988, the Soviet Union's government began a steady decline in control and structure. The decline led to a final collapse in 1991 when a coup brought Boris Yeltsin to power after toppling Gorbachev. One cannot help but wonder why the military was not more involved in the struggle. After all, for a hundred years, all the coups in Russia had included the military. Why were they not more active this time?

Some might suggest that the military had not gotten involved in the transfer of power in Russia because they had been converted to democracy, but that conclusion lacks logic. Perhaps, just perhaps there is another reason. What if the loss of Soviet 7 was a major military demoralizer? What if the loss of Soviet 7 so tipped the balance of military power that the Russian military machine became impotent? What if the loss of Soviet 7 was a silent factor by stunning the Soviet military machine? What if?

Oh, by the way, a ninth name now decorates the plaque of "Meritorious Distinction in Satellite Reconnaissance". The name—Jesse W. Webb, 1988.

THE END